Same Time, Next Year

A COMEDY IN TWO ACTS

By Bernard Slade

SAMUEL FRENCH, INC.

45 WEST 25TH STREET   NEW YORK 10010
7623 SUNSET BOULEVARD   HOLLYWOOD 90046
LONDON   TORONTO

DISCARD

SAME TIME, NEXT YEAR was first performed March 13, 1975 at the Brooks Atkinson Theatre, New York, N. Y. It was produced by Morton Gottlieb, Dasha Epstein, and Edward L. Schuman. Directed by Gene Saks, Associate Producer Ben Rosenberg and Warren Crane. Scenery by William Ritman, Costumes by Jane Greenwood, and Lighting by Tharon Musser. The cast was as follows:

CAST

DORIS .... *Ellen Burstyn*

GEORGE .... *Charles Grodin*

SETTING

The entire action of the play takes place in a guest cottage of a country inn in Northern California.

ACT ONE

SCENE 1: A day in February, 1951

SCENE 2: A day in February, 1956

SCENE 3: A day in February, 1961

ACT TWO

SCENE 1: A day in February, 1965

SCENE 2: A day in February, 1970

SCENE 3: A day in February, 1975

DATE DUE

JAN 3 2007	
JAN 5 2009	

Same Time, Next Year

ACT ONE

SCENE 1

THE TIME: *A day in February, 1951.*

THE PLACE: *A bed-sitting room in the cottage of a Spanish style inn near Mendecino, North of San Francisco. It is a cozy comfortable room, large enough to contain a double bed, dressing table, chintz-covered sofa, a baby grand piano, wood burning fireplace and an ottoman. There are two leaded pane glass windows, a closet, a door leading to the bathroom and another door which opens onto the patio-entrance to the cottage. The room's aura of permanence is not an illusion. The decor has been the same for the past twenty-five years and will not change for the next twenty-five.*

AT RISE: GEORGE *and* DORIS *are in bed.* GEORGE *is sitting up against the headboard of the bed rigidly staring into space.* DORIS *is lying in a sleeping position but her eyes are wide open. Very slowly and carefully* GEORGE *gets out of the bed. When she feels* GEORGE *move,* DORIS *shuts her eyes and pretends to be asleep.* GEORGE *picks up his jacket and puts it on, then he finds a sock and puts that on. As he is putting on the second sock* DORIS *turns to watch him.*

DORIS. That's a real sharp looking outfit.
GEORGE. Hello.
DORIS. Hi.

5

GEORGE. Did I wake you?

DORIS. I was awake.

GEORGE. How'd you sleep?

DORIS. Fine, thank you. (DORSI *reaches for her petticoat which is on the dressing table stool beside the bed. She pulls it under the sheet and puts the sheet over her head while she gets into her slip.* GEORGE *meanwhile has found his trousers and quickly puts them on.*) What time is it?

GEORGE. My watch is on the bedside table.

DORIS. (*Picks up watch.*) Ten to twelve!

GEORGE. No, it's twenty-five after eight. The stem is broken. It's three hours and twenty-five minutes fast.

DORIS. Why don't you get it fixed?

GEORGE. I was going to. I got used to it.

DORIS. Doesn't it mix you up?

GEORGE. No, I'm very quick with figures.

DORIS. Why are you looking at me like that?

GEORGE. We're in a lot of trouble.

DORIS. Yeah?

GEORGE. Why do you have to look so luminous? It would make it a lot easier if you woke up with puffy eyes and blotchy skin like everyone else.

DORIS. I guess God figured chubby thighs were enough.

GEORGE. Look, this is not just going to go away. We've got to talk about it.

DORIS. Okay. (*She gets out of bed, the sheet around her, and starts for the bathroom.*)

GEORGE. Where are you going?

DORIS. I'm going to brush my teeth.

GEORGE. Dorothy, please sit down. (DORIS *starts to speak.*) Please sit down and let me say this. (*She sits on the end of the bed.*) Dorothy, first of all, I want you to know last night was the most beautiful, wonderful, crazy thing that's ever happened to me and I'll never forget it—or you.

DORIS. Doris.

GEORGE. What?

Doris. My name is Doris.

George. Your name is Doris. I've been calling you Dorothy all night. Why didn't you tell me earlier?

Doris. I didn't expect us to end up like we did. Then I did try to tell you but you weren't listening.

George. When?

Doris. Right in the middle of everything.

George. It was incredible wasn't it?

Doris. It was—nice. Especially the last time.

George. I'm an animal. I don't know what got into me. What was the matter with the first two times?

Doris. What? Oh—well, the first time was kinda fast and the second—look, I feel funny talking about this.

George. It was a very beautiful thing, Doris. There was nothing disgusting or dirty in what we did.

Doris. Then how come you look so down in the dumps?

George. My wife is going to kill me.

Doris. How is she going to find out?

George. She knows.

Doris. You said she was in New Jersey.

George. It doesn't matter. She knows.

Doris. How?

George. Was it as incredible for you as it was for me?

Doris. Do all men like to talk about it a lot afterwards?

George. Why? You think I'm some sort of pervert or something?

Doris. No, I just wondered. See, I was a virgin when I got married. At least sort of.

George. Sort of?

Doris. Well, I was pregnant but I don't count that.

George. Doris, that counts.

Doris. I mean it was by the man I married.

George. Oh, I'm sorry.

Doris. (*She is putting on her blouse.*) That's okay. Harry and me would've gotten married anyway. It just speeded things up a bit. Turns out I get pregnant if we drink from the same cup. (*He looks at her.*) What's the matter?

GEORGE. It's okay. Trojans are very reliable.

DORIS. Who are?

GEORGE. Never mind. I'm in a lot of trouble. I think I love you. It's crazy! It's really crazy! I don't even know if you've read "Catcher in the Rye".

DORIS. I didn't graduate high school.

GEORGE. You see? I don't even care! Of course, I should've known this would happen. There's something about me I didn't tell you.

DORIS. What? (*She puts on her skirt.*)

GEORGE. When it comes to life I have a brown thumb.

DORIS. What do you mean?

GEORGE. Nothing I do ever turns out right. Ever. The first time I had sex I was eighteen years old. We were in the back seat of a parked 1938 Dodge sedan. Right in the middle of it we were rear ended.

DORIS. Gee, that's terrible. Did you have insurance?

GEORGE. You know the song they were playing on the juke box last night when we met?

DORIS. No?

GEORGE. "If I Knew You Were Coming I'd've Baked A Cake"!

DORIS. So?

GEORGE. So that's going to be "our song"! Other people would get "Be My Love" or "Hello Young Lovers". Me—I get "If I Knew You Were Coming I'd've Baked A Cake"!

DORIS. You're very romantic. I like that.

GEORGE. I think I'm in love with you. Now you want to know the luck I have? I'm happily married!

DORIS. Are you Jewish?

GEORGE. No.

DORIS. Well, how come you're so guilty?

GEORGE. Don't you feel guilty?

DORIS. Are you kidding? Half my high school became nuns.

GEORGE. Catholics have rules about this sort of thing.

DORIS. We have rules about everything. That's what's so great about being Catholic. You always know where you stand.

GEORGE. I tell you, Doris, I feel like slitting my wrists.

DORIS. Are you Italian?

GEORGE. What's with you and nationalities?

DORIS. You're so emotional.

GEORGE. I happen to be a C.P.A. I can be as logical as the next person.

DORIS. You don't strike me as an accountant type.

GEORGE. It's very simple. My whole life has been a mess. Figures always come out right. I like that. What are you?

DORIS. I'm Italian.

GEORGE. Why aren't you more emotional?

DORIS. When you grow up in a large Italian family, it's enough to turn you off emotion for life.

GEORGE. I wondered why you weren't crying or yelling.

DORIS. I did before in the bathroom.

GEORGE. Crying?

DORIS. Yelling.

GEORGE. I didn't hear you.

DORIS. I stuffed a towel in my mouth.

GEORGE. I'm sorry.

DORIS. That's all right. There's no sense crying over spilt milk.

GEORGE. You're right.

DORIS. Then how come we feel so terrible?

GEORGE. Because we're two decent, honest people and this thing is tearing us apart. I mean I know it wasn't our fault but I keep seeing the faces of my children and the look of betrayal in their eyes. I keep thinking of our marriage vows, the trust my wife has placed in me, the experiences we've shared together. And you know the worst part of it all? While I'm thinking of all these things, I have this fantastic hard on.

DORIS. I really wish you hadn't said that.

GEORGE. I'm sorry. I just feel we should be totally honest with each other.

DORIS. No, it's not that. I have to go to confession.

GEORGE. We're both crazy! I mean this sort of thing happens to millions of people every day. We're just normal, healthy human beings who did a perfectly healthy, normal thing. You don't use actual names in confession do you?

DORIS. No.

GEORGE. May I ask you something?

DORIS. Sure.

GEORGE. Would you go to bed with me again?

DORIS. George, we can't!

GEORGE. Why not?

DORIS. We'll feel worse afterwards!

GEORGE. No. I'm over that now; I just remembered something!

DORIS. What?

GEORGE. The Russians have the bomb! We could all be dead tomorrow!

DORIS. George, you're clutching at straws!

GEORGE. Don't you understand? We're both grown up people who have absolutely nothing to be ashamed or afraid of!!!! (*There is a KNOCK at the door. They both freeze.*) Just a second! (*Then they go into frantic action. He attempts to straighten up the room. She grabs her hat, jacket, purse and starts for the bathroom.*) Don't go into the bathroom!

DORIS. Why not?

GEORGE. It's the first place they look! Just a second! I'm coming! (*She heads for the window and climbs out. He spots her girdle on the hearth, grabs it and stuffs it part way into his pocket. He opens the door about six inches and squeezes outside, closing the door behind him. We hear a muffled exchange Offstage before he reenters carrying a breakfast tray which*

he places on the coffee table. He looks around for
Doris, *sees open window and crosses to it.*) Doris?
Doris? (*While he is looking out the window, she
comes through the front door.*)

Doris. You have a woman in here?

George. (*Startled, he turns to face her.*) It's okay.
I was very calm. It was old Mr. Chalmers with my
breakfast. He didn't suspect a thing.

Doris. He didn't ask about your girdle?

George. What girdle? (*He looks at his pocket, and
sees her girdle.*) Oh, great! Now he probably thinks
I'm a homo!

Doris. (*She takes the girdle and puts it into her
purse.*) What do you care?

George. I stay here every year.

Doris. You do, why?

George. I have a friend who went into the wine
business near here. I fly out the same weekend every
year to do his books.

Doris. From New Jersey?

George. He was my first client. It's kind of a
sentimental thing.

Doris. Oh.

George. Doris, there's something I want to tell you.

Doris. What?

George. I know I must appear very smooth and
glib—sexually. Well, I want you to know that since
I've been married this is the very first time I've done
this.

Doris. Don't worry, I could tell. Do you mind if I
have some of your breakfast?

George. Go ahead. I'm not hungry. It's funny when
I was single I was no good at quick, superficial affairs.
I had to be able to really like the person before . . .
What do you mean—you could tell? In what way could
you tell?

Doris. What? Oh—I don't know—the way you tried
to get your pants off over your shoes and then tripped

and hit your head on the coffee table. Little things like that.

GEORGE. It's great to be totally honest with another person isn't it?

DORIS. It sure is.

GEORGE. I haven't been totally honest with you.

DORIS. No?

GEORGE. No. I told you I was a married man with two children.

DORIS. You're not?

GEORGE. No. I'm a married man with three children. I thought it would make me seem less married. Look, I just didn't think it through. Anyway, it's been like a lead weight inside me all morning. I mean denying little Debbie like that. I don't normally behave like this, I was under a certain stress. You understand?

DORIS. Sure, we all do dopey things sometimes. How come your wife doesn't travel with you?

GEORGE. Phyliss won't get on a plane.

DORIS. Is she afraid of flying?

GEORGE. Crashing.

DORIS. (*Noticing that* GEORGE *is staring at her.*) Why are you looking at me like that?

GEORGE. I love the way you eat.

DORIS. You wanta share some coffee with me?

GEORGE. No thank you. Doris, do you believe that two perfect strangers can look at each other across a crowded room and suddenly want to possess each other in every conceivable way possible?

DORIS. No.

GEORGE. Then how did this whole thing start?

DORIS. It started when you sent me over that steak in the restaurant.

GEORGE. They didn't serve drinks. They're known for their steaks.

DORIS. Then when I looked over and you toasted me with your fork with a big piece of steak on it, that really made me laugh. I never saw anybody do that before. What made you do it?

GEORGE. Impulse. Usually I never do that sort of thing. I have a friend who says that life is saying "yes". The most I've ever been able to manage is "maybe".

DORIS. So then why did you do it?

GEORGE. I was lonely and you looked so vulnerable. You had a run in your stocking and your lipstick was smeared.

DORIS. You thought I looked cheap?

GEORGE. I thought you looked beautiful.

DORIS. I really should be going. The nuns will be wondering what happened to me.

GEORGE. Nuns?

DORIS. Yeah. It didn't seem right to bring up when we met yesterday in the restaurant but I was on my way to retreat.

GEORGE. Retreat?

DORIS. It's right near here. I go every year at this time when Harry takes the kids to Bakersfield.

GEORGE. What's in Bakersfield?

DORIS. His mother. It's her birthday.

GEORGE. She doesn't mind that you don't go?

DORIS. No, she hates me.

GEORGE. Why?

DORIS. I got pregnant.

GEORGE. Her son had something to do with that.

DORIS. She blocks that out of her mind. You see, he was in his first year of dental college and he had to quit and take a job selling waterless cooking. And so now every year on her birthday I go on retreat.

GEORGE. To think about God?

DORIS. Well, Him too, sure. See I have three little kids. I got pregnant the first time when I was eighteen and so I never really had any time to think about what I think. Never mind . . . sometimes I think I'm crazy.

GEORGE. Why?

DORIS. Well, take my life. I live in a two bedroom duplex in downtown Oakland, we have a 1948 Kaiser, a blond three piece dinette set, Motorola TV, and we go bowling at least once a week. I mean what else could anyone ask for? But sometimes things get me down, you know? It's dumb!

GEORGE. I don't think it's dumb.

DORIS. You don't? Boy, I can really talk to you. It's amazing I find myself saying things to you that I didn't know I thought. I noticed that yesterday right after we met in the restaurant.

GEORGE. We had instant rapport! Did you notice that too?

DORIS. No, but I know we really hit it off. Harry's not much of a talker. How about your wife. Do you two talk a lot?

GEORGE. Doris, naturally we're both curious about each other's husband and wife. But rather than dwelling on it and letting it spoil everything why don't we do this. I'll tell you two stories one showing the best side of my wife and the other showing the worst. Then you do the same about your husband and then let's forget that. Okay?

DORIS. Okay.

GEORGE. I'll go first. I'll start with the worst side. Phyliss knows about us.

DORIS. Now you said that before. How could she know?

GEORGE. She has this thing in her head.

DORIS. Oh, you mean like a plate?

GEORGE. Plate?

DORIS. My uncle has one of those. He was wounded in the war and they put this steel plate in his head and now he says he can always tell when it's going to rain.

GEORGE. I'm in a lot of trouble.

DORIS. Why?

GEORGE. I find everything you say absolutely fascinating.

DORIS. Tell me about your wife's steel plate.

GEORGE. No, it's not a plate—it's more like a bell. I

could be a million miles away but if I even look at
another girl she knows it. Last night at 1:22 I just
know she sat bolt upright in bed with her head going,
ding, ding, ding, ding!

Doris. How'd you know it was 1:22?

George. My watch said 4:47.

Doris. Okay, now tell me a story about the good
side of her.

George. Well. She helped me believe in myself. I
mean, it may be hard for you to imagine but I used to
be very insecure.

Doris. How did she do that? Help you believe in
yourself?

George. She married me.

Doris. That was very nice of her. I mean bolstering
you up and all.

George. Okay, your turn. Tell me the worst story
first.

Doris. Okay. (*Pause.*) It's hard.

George. To pick one?

Doris. No, to think of one. Harry's the salt of the
earth—everyone says so.

George. Look, you owe me at least one rotten story.

Doris. Okay. This is not really rotten but well—
It was on our fourth anniversary. We were having kind
of a rough time. I was pregnant and we'd gotten in
over our heads financially but we decided to have some
people over to help celebrate. Now Harry doesn't
drink much but he did have three beers that night. It
was after the Gillette fights and I overheard him talking to some of the guys and he said his time in the
Army were the best years of his life.

George. A lot of guys feel that way about the
service.

Doris. Harry was in the Army four years. Three of
those years were spent in a Japanese prison camp!
And he said this on our anniversary. Oh, I know he
didn't mean to hurt me—Harry would never hurt

anyone—but, well, it hurt, you know? Promise me you won't ever tell anybody I told you that.

GEORGE. I wouldn't tell anybody.

DORIS. Because I never told anyone that before. Now, you wanta hear a story about the good side of him?

GEORGE. Not really.

DORIS. You have to! I don't want you to get the wrong impression of him.

GEORGE. Okay, if you insist.

DORIS. Well, Harry's a real big, heavyset sort of guy.

GEORGE. I wish you hadn't told me that.

DORIS. Oh, no, he's gentle as a puppy. Anyway he tries to do different things with each of the kids, you know? So, he was having a hard time finding something special to do with Tony, our four year old. Then he gets the idea to take him out to fly a kite. So this one Saturday last winter they go out but there's no wind and they have trouble getting the kite to take off. Well, after a while Tony who's pretty bored by now, he's only four years old, asks if he can go sit in the car. Harry said "okay." (*She starts to laugh.*) About an hour later I come by on my way home from the laundromat and I see Tony sound asleep in the car and Harry all alone in the park, all red in the face and out of breath pounding up and down with this huge kite dragging along behind him. (*She sees that* GEORGE *is not laughing.*) Well, it really got to me.

GEORGE. Yeah, I know. Helen has some wonderful qualities too.

DORIS. Who's Helen?

GEORGE. My wife.

DORIS. You said her name was Phyliss.

GEORGE. I lied. Phyliss—Helen—what's the difference? I'm married. I'm sorry I didn't want to leave any clues. I thought you might try to look me up or something.

DORIS. Is your name really George?

GEORGE. My name? Do you think I'd lie about my own name?

DORIS. Yes.

GEORGE. That'd be crazy.

DORIS. You're crazy.

GEORGE. It's funny, isn't it? Here we are in a hotel room, gazing into each other's eyes, and we're married with six kids between us.

DORIS. You got pictures?

GEORGE. What?

DORIS. Pictures of your kids.

GEORGE. Well, sure, but I don't think this is the time or place to . . .

DORIS. I'll show you mine if you show me yours. (*She takes folder from her purse.*) I keep them in a special folder we got free from Kodak. Where are yours?

GEORGE. (*Reluctantly takes out his wallet.*) You have to take the whole wallet. (*They sit side by side on the sofa.*)

DORIS. Oh, they're cute! Is that the oldest one in the glasses and baggy tights?

GEORGE. That's Michael. Funny looking kid isn't he?

DORIS. Does he want to be Superman?

GEORGE. Peter Pan. Sometimes it worries me. (*Looking at snap in his hand.*) Why is this one's face all scrunched up?

DORIS. Oh, that's Paul. It was taken on a roller coaster. Isn't it natural looking? Right after that he threw up.

GEORGE. Yeah, he's really something. I guess he looks like Harry, huh?

DORIS. Both of us really. What's your little girl's name?

GEORGE. Debbie. That was taken on her second birthday. We were trying to get her to blow out the candles.

DORIS. She has her hand in the cake.

GEORGE. Yeah, neat is not her strong suit.

DORIS. You have great looking kids, George.

GEORGE. Thank you. So do you.

DORIS. Thank you. (*They hand back the photographs which each immediately replaces where they came from. They gaze at one another, move into an awkward embrace which becomes extremely passionate. They pull apart. Removing her hat and rising.*) Okay. But this is the last time.

CURTAIN

END OF SCENE 1

ACT ONE

SCENE 2

THE TIME: *A day in February, 1956.*

THE PLACE: *The same.*

AT RISE: GEORGE *has just hung a* HAPPY 5th *sign on the front door.* DORIS *is Offstage in the bathroom changing.* GEORGE *takes a small cake from the bedside table and puts it with two plates and forks on the coffee table.*

DORIS. (*Offstage.*) Damn.

GEORGE. What?

DORIS. (*Offstage.*) It's my merry widow.

GEORGE. Your what?

DORIS. (*Offstage.*) Merry widow. It mashes you in and pushes you out in all the right places. But it cuts off all circulation so you can't breathe.

GEORGE. Be sure and let me know when you're coming out.

DORIS. (*Offstage.*) Right now.

GEORGE. Wait a minute! (*He sits at piano.*) Okay—now! (*He plays and sings "IF I KNEW YOU WERE COMIN' I'DA BAKED A CAKE" as she enters.*) Happy anniversary, darling. (*He hands her a glass of champagne and they toast.*) Cut the cake and make a wish. (DORIS *crosses to sit on sofa to cut cake.*) What did you wish?

DORIS. I only have one wish.

GEORGE. What?

DORIS. That you keep showing up every year.

GEORGE. That was one of the best ideas you ever had.

DORIS. What? That we meet here every year. I don't think either one of us can take credit for that. It was just something we stumbled into. Matter of fact, that first year I didn't think you'd show up at all.

GEORGE. I was sure you wouldn't. Of course, in those days I had less confidence in my personal magnetism.

DORIS. Where'd you get the champagne?

GEORGE. Old Chalmers brought it while you were changing.

DORIS. Bit risky, isn't it?

GEORGE. I'm sure by now old Chalmers knows the score.

DORIS. I really think he does. Everytime I go past the front desk he winks at me.

GEORGE. That's not a wink. He has a tic in his eye.

DORIS. Chalmers has a tic? Why didn't you tell me that before. For five years I've been winking back! (*Pause . . .* GEORGE *stares at* DORIS.) What? You hate my hair, don't you?

GEORGE. I've already told you I'm crazy about your hair.

DORIS. It's not too blonde? I don't know, maybe next time I should go into the city to have it done.

GEORGE. How are the suburbs?

DORIS. Muddy mostly. Right now everyone's very excited. Next week they're going to connect the sewers. Well, it's not exactly the life of Scott and Zelda, but we're surviving.

GEORGE. You started reading.

DORIS. Oh, you don't know the half of it. I joined the Book of the Month Club.

GEORGE. Good for you.

DORIS. Sometimes I even take the alternate selections. How about you? You still in New Jersey?

GEORGE. We moved to Connecticut. We bought an old barn and converted it.

DORIS. How is it?

GEORGE. Drafty. Helen's got the decorating bug. I have this mental picture of her at my funeral just as they're closing the lid on my coffin she'll throw in two fabric swatches and yell out, "Which one do you like?" That's the bad story about her.

DORIS. What else is new?

GEORGE. We had a baby girl.

DORIS. Oh, congratulations! You have pictures?

GEORGE. I knew you'd ask.

DORIS. Oh, she's adorable. It's funny. I still like to look at babies but I don't want to own one anymore. You think that's a sign of maturity?

GEORGE. Could be. (*He takes out cigar.*) Here, I even kept one of these for you to give to Harry. It's from Havana.

DORIS. Harry still thinks I go on retreat. What should I tell him? It came from a Cuban nun! (*He takes the cigar back.*) How are the rest of the kids? How's Michael?

GEORGE. Oh, crazy as ever. He had this homework assignment, to write what he did on his summer vacation. Trouble is, he chose to write what he actually did.

DORIS. What was that?

GEORGE. Tried to get laid. He wrote in great comic detail about his unfortunate tendency to get an erection on all forms of public transportation. The school almost suspended him.

DORIS. You're crazy about him, aren't you?

GEORGE. He's a very weird kid, Doris.

DORIS. And he really gets to you. Come on—admit it.

GEORGE. O.K. I admit it. He's a nice kid. (*He kisses her.*)

DORIS. What was that for?

GEORGE. Everything. This. One beautiful weekend every year with no cares, no ties and no responsibilities. Thank you, Doris. (*They go into a passionate embrace.*)

DORIS. Gee, I just got all dressed up.

(*They move toward the bed, stop for a final embrace which carries them on to the bed. Just at that moment the phone rings.*)

GEORGE. (*Reaches out and picks up phone.*) Hello. Yes. (*He sits up.*) Yes, this is Daddy. Is everything all right? It came out huh? Which one was it? Of course the tooth-fairy will come, sweetheart. Why tonight, of course. It doesn't matter if you can't find it darling, the tooth-fairy will know. Well, I wish I could be there to find it for you too, honey, but Daddy's working. Oh, in my room. Honey, does Mommy know you're calling? Well I'm sure she'll be back any minute. Yes it's a very nice room . . . well, it has a fireplace and a sofa and a big comfortable b . . . bathroom. I wish I could be there to help you find it too sweetheart but Daddy has to finish his business. Yes, I love you too, sweetheart. Goodbye . . . goodbye. (*He hangs up.*) Oh, I feel so guilty!

DORIS. Debbie?

GEORGE. Her tooth came out. She can't find it and she's afraid the tooth-fairy won't know. That thin reedy, little voice. Do you know what that does to me!

DORIS. Sure, that cheerful look on your face doesn't fool me for a minute.

GEORGE. You think this is funny?

DORIS. Honey, I understand how you feel but I really don't think it's going to help going on about it.

GEORGE. Doris, my little girl calls me on the phone and says, "I love you, Daddy," and I answered her with a voice still hoarse with passion!

Doris. I get the picture, George.

George. Don't you ever feel any guilt?

Doris. Sometimes.

George. You never say anything.

Doris. I just handle it in a different way.

George. How?

Doris. Privately.

George. I think in some ways men are more sensitive than women.

Doris. Would you like some more champagne, dear?

George. I mean women are more pragmatic than men.

Doris. What do you mean?

George. They adjust to rottenness quicker. Anyway, you have the church.

Doris. The Church?

George. You're Catholic. You can get rid of your guilt all at one sitting. I have to live with mine.

Doris. There's a lot about being Catholic you don't understand.

George. I tell you, when she started talking about the tooth-fairy—well, it affected me in a very profound manner. On top of that I have indigestion you can't believe. It hit me hard, you know?

Doris. George, I have three children too.

George. Sure, sure—I know. I don't mean that you don't understand. It's just that I think that my guilt is more acute than yours.

Doris. Honey, what do you want to do? Have a guilt contest? Will that solve anything?

George. What do you want me to do, Doris?

Doris. I think it might be a terrific idea if you stopped talking about it. It's only making you feel worse.

George. I couldn't feel worse. My little girl calls me on the phone . . . that pure little voice saying . . . No, you're right. Forget it. Forget it. Talk about something else. Tell me the good story about Harry.

Doris. Okay. He went bankrupt.

GEORGE. How can anyone go bankrupt selling TV sets?

DORIS. Harry has one failing as a salesman. It's a compulsion to talk his customers out of things they can't afford. He lacks the killer instinct. Actually, it's one of the things I like best about him. Anyway, he went into real estate. Your turn.

GEORGE. What?

DORIS. Tell me your story about Helen.

GEORGE. I already did.

DORIS. You just told me the bad one. Why do you always tell that one first?

GEORGE. It's the one I look forward to telling the most.

DORIS. Tell me the good story about her.

GEORGE. Chris, our middle one, gashed his knee badly on the lawn sprinkler. Helen drove both of us to the hospital.

DORIS. Both of you?

GEORGE. I fainted. The nice part was she never told anybody.

DORIS. You faint often?

GEORGE. Only in emergencies.

DORIS. Is it the sight of blood that—

GEORGE. Please, Doris! My stomach's already squeamish. Oh, listen, something just occurred to me. Instead of leaving at my usual time would you mind if I left a little earlier?

DORIS. When did you have in mind?

GEORGE. Well, there's a plane in half an hour.

DORIS. You want to leave twenty-three hours early?

GEORGE. Look, I know how you feel, I really do, and I wouldn't even suggest it if you weren't a mother. I mean I wouldn't even think of it if this crisis hadn't come up. (*He moves his suitcase to the bed and starts packing through the following.*) Oh, it's not just the tooth-fairy but she could have swallowed the tooth. It could be lodged God knows where. Now I know this leaves you up in the air but there's no reason for you to leave too. The room's all paid for—have you seen my hairbrush? Anyway, I'm probably doing you a favor. If I did stay I wouldn't be very good company. (DORIS *throws the hairbrush at him. It sails past his head and crashes into the wall. There is a pause.*) You feel somewhat rejected right? I can understand that but I want you to know my leaving has nothing to do with you and me. Doris, I have a sick child at home. This is an emergency.

DORIS. Will you stop it. It's got nothing to do with the goddam tooth-fairy. You're just feeling guilty and the only way you think you can deal with it is by getting as far away from me as possible.

GEORGE. Okay, I feel guilty. Is that so strange? Doris, we're cheating! Once a year we lie to our families and sneak off to a hotel in California and commit adultery. Not that I want to stop doing it! But yes, I feel guilt. I admit it.

DORIS. You admit it! You take out ads. You probably stop strangers on the street. I'm surprised you haven't had a scarlet "A" embroidered on your jockey shorts? You think that by talking about it you can excuse what you're doing. So you wander around like an open nerve saying, "I'm cheating but look how guilty I feel so I must really be a nice guy"! And to top it all, you have the incredible arrogance to think you're the only one in the world with a conscience. Well, that doesn't make you a nice guy. You know what that makes you? A horse's ass.

GEORGE. You know something? I liked you a lot better before you joined the Book of the Month Club. Doris, it's not the end of the world. I'm not leaving permanently. I'll see you next year.

DORIS. No, I don't think you will.

GEORGE. I don't believe this. Just because I have to leave early one year you're willing to throw away a lifetime of weekends? How can you be so *casual?*

DORIS. I don't see any point in going on.

GEORGE. Oh, no. Don't do that to me, Doris. Don't

try to manipulate me. I get enough of that at home. That's not what our relationship is about.

DORIS. What is it about?

GEORGE. You don't know?

DORIS. Yes. But it seems to be completely different from what you think it's about. That's why I think we should stop seeing each other.

GEORGE. You're serious.

DORIS. George, what's the point of meeting in guilt and remorse? What joy is there in that?

GEORGE. Doris, I have a commitment there.

DORIS. And you have none here?

GEORGE. Here? I thought our only commitment was to show up every year.

DORIS. Just two friendly sex partners who meet once a year, touch and let go.

GEORGE. Okay. Maybe I was kidding myself. I'm human.

DORIS. Well, so am I.

GEORGE. But you're different. Stronger. You always seem able to cope.

DORIS. During the past year I picked up the phone and started to call you ten times. I couldn't seem to stop thinking about you. You kept slipping over into my real life and it bothered the hell out of me. More to the point I felt guilty. So I decided to stop seeing you. At first I wasn't going to show up at all but then I thought I at least owed you an explanation. So I came. When you walked in the door I knew I couldn't do it. That no matter what the price I'm willing to pay it.

GEORGE. Oh God, I feel so *guilty!*

DORIS. I think you'd better leave, George.

GEORGE. Doris, I love you. I'm an idiot, I suspect I'm deeply neurotic, and I'm no bargain—but I do love you. Will you let me stay? (*She turns to him and smiles. They move into each other's arms.*) What are we going to do?

DORIS. Touch and hold on very tight . . . until tomorrow.

THE CURTAIN FALLS

END ACT ONE, SCENE 2

ACT ONE

SCENE 3

THE TIME: *A day in February, 1961.*

THE PLACE: *The Same.*

AT RISE: GEORGE *is on the telephone. He has obviously just arrived. He still has his raincoat and hat on. His suitcase is sitting unopened at the foot of the bed* .

GEORGE. (*Into phone.*) No, of course I haven't left Helen. I'm on a business trip. I come out here every year—I am not running away from the problem. Of course I know it's serious. I still don't think it's any reason to phone me long distance and— Yes, I saw a doctor. He said it's no big deal. It happens to every man at one time or another. Look, if we have to discuss this you may as well pronounce it correctly. It's impotence, not im*po*tence. What do you mean, did I catch it in time? It's not a terminal illness, it's a slight reflex problem. It's not a question of nipping it in the bud. Look, how did you find out about this anyway? What sort of hints? You asked her and she looked funny. Terrific! Look I really don't want to discuss this. I'm going to be okay—soon—I just know, that's all. I'm seeing an expert out here! Look, I don't think we should even be *discussing* this! I'm sorry, I'm going to hang up now. Goodbye, Mother! (*He slams the* *receiver down. He opens his suitcase and takes out his pajamas and robe and exits into the bathroom. There is a slight pause and the front door opens to reveal an obviously pregnant* DORIS. *She crosses and puts her suitcase down by the bed. She goes to the bathroom door and calls out.*)

DORIS. George!

GEORGE. (*Offstage.*) Be right out, darling! (*DORIS crosses to the fireplace and with some difficulty lights the fire. She is standing facing Downstage with her back to the bathroom door when* GEORGE *comes out of the bathroom wearing his pajamas and robe.*) How are you lover? (*She turns to face him revealing her pregnancy.* GEORGE *is dumbfounded. He sinks slowly onto the hassock.*)

DORIS. Guess what?

GEORGE. What have you done to yourself?

DORIS. Well, I can't take all the credit. It was a mutual effort. Honey, when you haven't seen an old friend for a year isn't it customary to kiss them hello?

GEORGE. Yes, of course. (*He gives her a kiss.*)

DORIS. Are you okay, pal?

GEORGE. I'm fine. I'm a little surprised.

DORIS. You're surprised. I insisted on visiting the dead rabbit's grave! George, how come you're in your pajamas and robe in the afternoon?

GEORGE. I'm rehearsing a Noel Coward play.

DORIS. George, is there something on your mind?

GEORGE. Not anymore. You must be eight months pregnant!

DORIS. Exactly. Honey, it's not that tragic. We'll just have to find some other way to communicate.

GEORGE. Great! You have any ideas?

DORIS. We could talk.

GEORGE. Talk I can get at home!

DORIS. Well, sex I can get at home. And as you can see, that ain't just talk.

GEORGE. What is that supposed to make me?

DORIS. What's the matter?

GEORGE. Matter? I'm the only man in America who just kept an illicit assignation with a woman who looks like a frigate in full sail. What was that crack about sex at home? Is that supposed to reflect on me? You don't think I have normal desires and sex drives?

DORIS. Of course I do. I think you're very normal. I just meant I look forward to this weekend all year for a lot of reasons besides sex. I just love being here, don't you?

GEORGE. Of course I do. Of course. You drive all the way up here in your condition and then I behave like a ridiculous idiot. I'm very sorry. You should have thrown something at me. I'm sorry.

DORIS. Is something else bothering you?

GEORGE. No, it's nothing I really want to talk about.

DORIS. Well, every year we meet it's a bit awkward at first but we usually solve that with a lot of heavy breathing between the sheets.

GEORGE. Honey, if we're not going to do it, would you mind not talking about it?

DORIS. I just meant maybe we need something else to break the ice.

GEORGE. I'm wide open to suggestions.

DORIS. How about this? I'll tell you some secret about myself I've never told anyone before and then you do the same.

GEORGE. I think I've had enough surprises for one day but go ahead.

DORIS. You'll like this one. I've been having sex dreams about you.

GEORGE. When?

DORIS. Just lately. Almost every night.

GEORGE. What sort of sex dreams?

DORIS. That's what's so strange. They're always the same. We're making love but always under water. In caves, grottos, swimming pools but always under water. Isn't that weird? Probably something to do with me being pregnant.

GEORGE. Under water, huh?

Doris. Now you tell me some deep, dark secret about yourself.

George. I can't swim.

Doris. Do you mean literally?

George. Of course literally! When I tell you I can't swim I simply mean I can't swim.

Doris. Okay, I just asked. How come?

George. I just never learned when I was a kid. Helen found out when she pushed me off a dock and I almost drowned but my kids don't even know. When we go to the beach I pretend I'm having trouble with my trick knee.

Doris. You have a trick knee?

George. No. They don't know that either.

Doris. You see, it worked. Now we're talking just like two people who have made love and everything. (*She moves to the other end of the couch and puts her feet up.*) Boy, I'll tell you something, that Ethel Kennedy must really like kids.

George. Hey, I'm really sorry about before. I'm very happy to see you.

Doris. Don't you want to tell me what's on your mind?

George. Okay, I may as well get it out in the open. It's nothing to be ashamed of. It's my sex life. Lately Helen hasn't been able to satisfy me.

Doris. She's lost her interest in sex?

George. Oh, she tries—God knows. But I can tell she's just going through the motions.

Doris. Do you have any idea why this is?

George. Well, Helen's always had a lot of hang-ups about sex. She's always thought of it as a healthy, normal, pleasant function. Don't you think that's a little bit twisted?

Doris. Only if you're Catholic.

George. You're joking but there's a lot to be said for guilt and shame. I think if you don't feel a certain amount of guilt you're missing half the fun. To Helen sex has always been good, clean entertainment. No wonder she grew tired of it. Anyway, for some reason my sex drive has increased while hers has decreased.

DORIS. That's odd. Usually, it's the other way around.

GEORGE. (*Defensively.*) Are you accusing me of lying?

DORIS. Of course not. Why are you so edgy?

GEORGE. Naturally I feel funny talking about this when she's not here to defend herself.

DORIS. Would you like to get to the more formal part of your presentation?

GEORGE. About Helen?

DORIS. Yes.

GEORGE. Okay. I'll start with the good story about her.

DORIS. You've never done that before. You must be mellowing.

GEORGE. Doris, do you mind? We went to London. We were checking into a hotel and there was a man in a formal coat and striped trousers standing at the front entrance. Helen handed him her suitcases and breezed on into the lobby. The man followed her and very politely pointed out that not only didn't he work at the hotel but that he was the Danish Ambassador. Without batting an eye she said, "Well, that's marvelous. Now you can tell us the best restaurants in Copenhagen." And he did. The point is it doesn't bother her when she makes a total ass of herself. I really admire that.

DORIS. And what is it that you don't admire?

GEORGE. That damned sense of humor of hers!

DORIS. Oh, good these are the stories I like the best.

GEORGE. We'd come home from a party and we'd had a few drinks and we went to bed and we started to make love. Well, nothing happened—for me—I couldn't— Well, you get the picture. It was no big deal. We laughed about it. Then about half an hour later, just as I was about to fall asleep she said, "It's funny, when I married a C.P.A. I always thought it would be his eyes that would go first."

DORIS. She was just trying to make you feel better.

GEORGE. Well, it didn't. Some things aren't that funny. I suppose what I'm trying to say is that the thing that bugs me most about Helen is that she broke my pecker!

DORIS. You're impotent?

GEORGE. Slightly. Okay, now five people know. You, me, Helen and her mother.

DORIS. Who's the fifth?

GEORGE. Chet Huntley. I'm sure her mother gave him a bulletin for the six o'clock news.

DORIS. When did it happen, honey?

GEORGE. Happen? Doris, we're not talking about a thruway accident! I mean you don't wake up one morning and say, "Oh, shoot, the old family jewels have gone on the blink." It's a gradual thing.

DORIS. And you really blame Helen for it?

GEORGE. Of course not. I just couldn't think of a graceful way to bring it up. I was just waiting for you to say "What's new?". And I was going to say, "Nothing, but I can tell you what's old."

DORIS. How's Helen reacting?

GEORGE. Oh, we don't discuss it much but I get the feeling she regards it as a lapse in my social responsibility. You know, rather like letting your partner down in tennis by not holding your serve. Seriously, I'll be okay. The patient's not dead. Just resting. (*She extends her hand.*) Doris, that statement hardly calls for congratulations.

DORIS. I need help getting up. (*He helps her get up from the couch.*) Honey, I'm really sorry. Is there anything I can say that will make you feel any better?

GEORGE. You can say anything you want except "it's all in your head." I mean, I'm no doctor but I have a great sense of direction. Look, to tell you the truth, I'm not too crazy about the whole subject. Let's forget it, huh?

DORIS. Okay. What do you want to talk about?

GEORGE. Anything but sex. How'd you feel about being pregnant?

DORIS. Catatonic, incredulous, angry, pragmatic, and finally maternal. Pretty much in that order.

GEORGE. Your vocabulary's improving.

DORIS. You don't know. You're talking to a high school graduate.

GEORGE. How come?

DORIS. Well, I was confined to bed for the first three months of my pregnancy so it shouldn't be a total loss I took a correspondence course.

GEORGE. You're really something you know that?

DORIS. There's kind of an ironic twist to all this.

GEORGE. What?

DORIS. Well, I didn't graduate from high school the first time because I got pregnant. And now I did graduate from high school because I got pregnant. Appeals to my sense of order.

GEORGE. I didn't know you had a sense of order.

DORIS. That's unfair. I'm much better at housework lately. Now I'm only two years behind in my ironing. Must be the nesting instinct. Anyway, the day my diploma came in the mail Harry bought me a big corsage and took me out dancing. Well, we didn't really dance—we lumbered. Afterwards we went to a malt shop and had a hot fudge sundae. That's this year's good story about Harry.

GEORGE. He still selling real estate?

DORIS. Insurance. He likes it. Gives him a chance to look up all his old army buddies.

GEORGE. Honey, are you comfortable in that position?

DORIS. When you're in my condition you're not comfortable in any position.

GEORGE. Why don't you sit up here you'll be more comfortable. (*He helps her move to the top of the bed where he has fixed the pillows for her to lean against. During the following he removes her shoes for her.*)

DORIS. Thank you. How are the kids?

GEORGE. Michael got a job with the Associated Press.

DORIS. Oh darling, that's marvelous. I'm so proud of him! (*She notices that he is staring at her.*) What?

GEORGE. What?

DORIS. Does my stomach offend you?

GEORGE. No, of course not. Tell me the other story about Harry.

DORIS. I had trouble getting up my nerve to tell him I was pregnant again. When I finally did he looked at me and said, "Well, there goes our old age." George, you're doing it again. What is it?

GEORGE. It's obscene.

DORIS. What is?

GEORGE. When I touched you I started to get excited! What kind of pervert am I? I'm staring at a two hundred pound pregnant woman and I'm getting hot!

DORIS. Well, I'll tell you something, that's the nicest thing anyone's said to me in months.

GEORGE. It's not funny.

DORIS. Aren't you pleased?

GEORGE. Pleased? I feel like I did on my seventh birthday. My uncle gave me fifty cents. I ran two miles and when I got there the candy store was closed!

DORIS. But doesn't this solve your problem?

GEORGE. The idea doesn't solve anything! It's the execution that counts.

DORIS. I really got to you, huh?

GEORGE. Excuse me. (*He crosses and sits at the piano and launches into Chopin's Revolutionary Etude No. 12. DORIS, surprised, gets up and comes to the piano.*)

DORIS. That's incredible. Are you as good as I think you are?

GEORGE. How good do you think I am?

DORIS. Sensational.

GEORGE. I'm not as good as you think I am.

DORIS. But that piano has been sitting there for ten years and you've hardly touched it. Why today?

GEORGE. It beats a cold shower.

DORIS. You play to release sexual tension?

GEORGE. You don't ever get this good without a lot of practice.

DORIS. You'll be exhausted.

GEORGE. That's the idea.

DORIS. I have a better idea. Come here. Come on.

GEORGE. (*He gets up from the piano as* DORIS *leads him toward the bed.*) Doris—

DORIS. It's okay. It'll be okay.

GEORGE. But you can't—

DORIS. I know that.

GEORGE. Then how—

DORIS. Don't worry, darling. We'll work something out. (*She kisses him and suddenly they are in a passionate embrace. Suddenly she doubles over in pain.*)

GEORGE. What? What is it? Doris? Doris, for God's sake, what is it? What's the matter?

DORIS. If memory serves me correctly I just had a labor pain.

GEORGE. You can't have! Maybe it's indigestion.

DORIS. No, there's a difference.

GEORGE. How can you be sure?

DORIS. Indigestion doesn't make your eyes bug out.

GEORGE. But you can't be in labor! When is the baby due?

DORIS. Not for another month.

GEORGE. My God, what have I done?

DORIS. What have *you* done?

GEORGE. I brought it on. My selfishness.

DORIS. You didn't have anything to do with it.

GEORGE. Don't treat me like a child, Doris!

DORIS. Will you stop getting so excited.

GEORGE. Excited? I thought I had troubles with my sex life before. Can you imagine what this is going to do to it.

DORIS. George, will you— (*She is stopped by a pain.*) I think I'd better lie down. (*She lies back on the bed.*)

GEORGE. What kind of man am I? What kind of man would do a thing like that?

DORIS. May I say something?

GEORGE. Look, I appreciate what you're trying to do, but nothing you can say will make me feel any better.

DORIS. I'm not trying to make you feel any better. I'm gonna have a baby.

GEORGE. I know that.

DORIS. No I mean now. I have a history of short labor.

GEORGE. Oh, no! Oh, no! How do you feel?

DORIS. Like I'm going to have a baby.

GEORGE. It's a false alarm. It's got to be a false alarm!

DORIS. Quiet down. Get on the phone and find out where the nearest hospital is.

GEORGE. Hospital? You want to go to a hospital?

DORIS. George, like it or not, I'm going to have a baby.

GEORGE. But we're not married! It's going to look odd!

DORIS. Will you get on the phone please.

GEORGE. Where are you going?

DORIS. The bathroom.

GEORGE. Why?

DORIS. No time to answer. (*She exits to the bathroom. He frantically picks up phone.*)

GEORGE. Hello, Mr. Chalmers? George Peterson. Er . . . ah. Where is the nearest hospital? It's my wife. Something unexpected came up. She got pregnant and now she's going to have the baby. That far . . . oh, my God! Get them on the phone for me, will you? (*He covers receiver with his hand.*) Doris! Doris! Doris, answer me!

DORIS. (*Offstage.*) I'm busy.

GEORGE. Yes, yes . . . hello, hello . . . hello I'm staying at the Sea Shadows Inn. I was in my room and I heard this groaning sound from the next room. So I looked in and saw this woman whom I'd never seen before in my life. It appears she's in labor. About three or four minutes apart. Hold on, I'll ask her. (*Hand over receiver, calling out.*) Doris, who's your doctor?

DORIS. (*Offstage.*) Joseph Harrington. Oakland 542-7878.

GEORGE. (*Into phone.*) Joseph Harrington. Oakland 542-7878. Yes, I have a car and I'd be happy to get her there— Right, right— Uh, could you answer one question? Would erotic contact during the last stages of pregnancy bring on premature . . . no reason, I just wondered. Right. I'll get her there. (*He hangs up, calls out.*) Doris, they're phoning your doctor. He'll meet us there at the hospital.

DORIS. (*Comes out of the bathroom.*) We're not going to make it to the hospital. My water just burst.

GEORGE. Oh, my God.

DORIS. We're going to have to find a doctor in the area.

GEORGE. What if we can't!?

DORIS. You look awful. You're not going to faint are you?

GEORGE. Doris, I'm not a cab driver! I don't know how to deliver babies!

DORIS. George, this is no time to start acting like Butterfly McQueen. Get the nearest doctor on the phone.

GEORGE. (*He races back to the phone.*) Mr. Chalmers . . . George. It's an emergency. Just get the nearest doctor in the area.

DORIS. This'll teach you to fool around with a married woman.

GEORGE. It's okay. Hold on, Doris, hold on. You're going to be okay. (*Into phone.*) Yes? His answering service! You don't understand. She's in the last stages of labor! Well, get in your car and drive down to the goddam golf course. Just get him! Get him. (*He hangs up.*) It's okay. He's on the golf course but it's just down the road. Chalmers is getting him. (DORIS *moans.*) What?

Doris. I feel the baby.

George. No!

Doris. George, I'm scared.

George. Lean back and relax.

Doris. George, do something!

George. I'll be right back. (*He exits into the bathroom.*)

Doris. George, don't leave me. Please I'm scared.

George. (*Offstage.*) I'm here, I'm here, honey.

Doris. George. (*He reappears with a pile of towels.*) What are those for?

George. Honey, we're going to have a baby.

Doris. We?

George. I'm going to need your help. Give me your hand. Look into my eyes. You're going to be fine. There's nothing to worry about, we're together. You think I play the piano well? Wait 'til you see the way I deliver babies.

CURTAIN

END ACT ONE, Scene 3

ACT TWO

Scene 1

The Time: *A day in February, 1965.*

The Place: *The Same.*

At Rise: George *is just finishing his unpacking. The last thing he takes out of his bag is a bottle of Chivas Regal which he takes to the tray on the piano and pours himself a drink. Drink in hand he crosses to the dressing table and takes his comb, keys and a prescription bottle out of his pocket and places them on the table.* Doris *enters in jeans, turtle neck, Indian necklace, headband, long hair and sandals.* George *is taken aback. They meet in an embrace.*

Doris. Hey, man! What do you say? So, you wanta fuck?

George. What?

Doris. You didn't understand the question?

George. Of course I did. I just think it's a damned odd way to start a conversation.

Doris. Yeah? I thought it would be a great little ice breaker. Aren't you horny after your long flight?

George. I didn't fly, I drove.

Doris. From Connecticut?

George. From Los Angeles. We moved to Beverly Hills about six months ago.

Doris. How come?

George. Oh, a lot of reasons. I got fed up standing kneedeep in snow trying to scrape the ice off my windshield with a credit card. Besides, there are a lot of

38

people out here with a lot of money who don't know what to do with it.

DORIS. And you tell them?

GEORGE. I'm what they call a Business Manager.

DORIS. How's it going?

GEORGE. I can't complain. Why?

DORIS. You look kinda shitty. Are you all right?

GEORGE. I'm fine.

DORIS. You sure?

GEORGE. When did you start dressing like an Indian? You look like a refugee from the Sunset Strip.

DORIS. I've gone back to school. Berkley.

GEORGE. Why?

DORIS. You mean what do I want to be when I grow up?

GEORGE. Well, you have to admit it's a bit odd becoming a schoolgirl at your age.

DORIS. Listen, you think it's easy being the only one in the class with clear skin.

GEORGE. What made you do it?

DORIS. It was a dinner party that made me decide. Harry's boss invited us over for dinner and I just freaked.

GEORGE. Why?

DORIS. I'd spent so much time with kids I didn't know if I was capable of carrying on an intelligent conversation with anyone over the age of five. Anyway, I went and was seated next to the boss. Well, I surprised myself. He talked—then I talked—you know, just like a real conversation. Everything was cool until I noticed him looking at me in a weird way. I looked down at his plate and realized that all the time we'd been talking I'd been cutting up his meat for him. That's when I decided I'd better get out of the house.

GEORGE. But why school?

DORIS. I felt restless and undirected and I thought school might give me some answers.

GEORGE. What sort of answers?

DORIS. Like where it's really at.

GEORGE. Jesus.

DORIS. What's the matter?

GEORGE. That expression.

DORIS. Okay. To find out who the hell I am.

GEORGE. You don't get those sort of answers from a classroom.

DORIS. I'm not in the classroom all the time. The protests and demonstrations are a learning experience in themselves.

GEORGE. Protests against what?

DORIS. The war of course. Didn't you hear about it? It was in all the papers.

GEORGE. Demonstrations aren't going to stop the war.

DORIS. You have a better idea?

GEORGE. Look, I didn't come up here to discuss politics.

DORIS. Well, so far you've turned down sex and politics. You want to try religion?

GEORGE. I think I'll try a librium.

DORIS. How come you're so uptight?

GEORGE. That's another expression I hate.

DORIS. Uptight?

GEORGE. There's no such word.

DORIS. You remind me of my mother when I was nine years old I asked her what "fuck" meant and do you know what she said? "There's no such word."

GEORGE. And now you've found out there is you feel compelled to use it in every other sentence?

DORIS. George, what's bugging you?

GEORGE. Bugging me? I'll tell you what's "bugging" me. The blacks are burning down the cities, there's a Harvard professor telling my kids the only way to happiness is to become doped up zombies, and I have a teenage son with hair so long that from the back he looks exactly like Yvonne deCarlo.

DORIS. That's right, honey. Let it all hang out.

GEORGE. I wish people would stop letting it "all

hang out." Especially my daughter. It's amazing she hasn't been arrested for indecent exposure.

DORIS. That's a sign of age, George.

GEORGE. What is?

DORIS. Being worried about the declining morality of the young. Besides, there's nothing you can do about it.

GEORGE. We could start by setting some examples.

DORIS. What do you want to do, George? Bring back public flogging?

GEORGE. It might not be a bad idea. We could start with the movie producers. My God, have you seen the movies lately? Half the time the audience achieves a climax before the movie does!

DORIS. It's natural for people to be interested in sex. You can't kid the body, George.

GEORGE. Maybe not but you can damn well be firm with it.

DORIS. As I recall when you were younger you weren't exactly a monk about that sort of thing.

GEORGE. That was different! Our relationship was not based upon a casual one night stand!

DORIS. No, it's been *fifteen* one night stands.

GEORGE. No it has not. We've shared things. My God, I helped deliver your child, remember?

DORIS. Remember? I consider it our finest hour.

GEORGE. How is she?

DORIS. Very healthy, very noisy, and very spoiled.

GEORGE. You don't feel guilty about leaving her alone while you're at school?

DORIS. Harry's home a lot. The insurance business hasn't been too good lately.

GEORGE. How does he feel about all this?

DORIS. When I told him I wanted to go back to school because I wanted some identity he said, "You want identity? Go build a bridge! Invent penicillin but get off my back!"

GEORGE. Harry always had a good head on his shoulders.

DORIS. George, that was supposed to be the *bad* story about him. How's Helen?

GEORGE. Helen's fine. Just fine.

DORIS. Tell me a story that shows how really rotten she can be.

GEORGE. That's not like you.

DORIS. It seems like we need something to bring us together. Maybe a bad story about Helen will make you appreciate me more.

GEORGE. Okay. Helen . . . As you know, she has this funny sense of humor.

DORIS. By funny I take it you mean peculiar?

GEORGE. Right. And it comes out at the most inappropriate times. I had signed this client—very proper, very old money. Helen and I were invited out to his house for cocktails to get acquainted with him and his wife. Well, it was all pretty awkward but we managed to get through the drinks all right. Then as we went to leave, instead of walking out the front door I walked into the hall closet. Now that's no big deal, right? I mean anybody can do that. The mistake I made was that I *stayed* in there.

DORIS. You stayed in the closet?

GEORGE. I wasn't sure they'd seen me go in. I thought I'd stay there until they'd gone away—okay? I was in there for about a minute before I realized I'd—well—misjudged the situation. When I came out the three of them were just staring at me. All right, it was an embarrassing situation but I probably could have carried it off. Except for what Helen did. You know what she did?

DORIS. What?

GEORGE. She peed on the carpet.

DORIS. She did *what?*

GEORGE. Oh, not right away. First, she started to laugh. Tears started to roll down her face. She held her sides. Then she peed all over their persian carpet.

DORIS. (*She laughs.*) What did you say?

GEORGE. I said, "You'll have to excuse my wife. Ever

since her last pregnancy she's had a problem." Then I offered to pay for the cleaning of the carpet.

DORIS. Did that help?

GEORGE. They said it wasn't necessary. They had a maid. You think this is funny?

DORIS. I've been meaning to tell you for a long time—I just love Helen.

GEORGE. Would she come off any worse if I told you I lost the account?

DORIS. George, when did you get so *stuffy?*

GEORGE. Stuffy? Am I stuffy is I don't like my wife to urinate on my client's carpets?

DORIS. I didn't mean just that but—well—look at you. I mean—you scream Establishment.

GEORGE. I am not a faddist!

DORIS. What do you mean?

GEORGE. I'm not going to be like those middle aged idiots with bell bottom trousers and Prince Valiant haircuts who go around yelling "Ciao!"

DORIS. I wasn't just talking about *fashion.* I was talking about your attitudes.

GEORGE. My attitudes are the same as they always were. I haven't changed.

DORIS. Yes, you have. You used to be green and insecure and a terrible liar and—human. Now you seem so sure of yourself.

GEORGE. That's the last thing I am.

DORIS. Oh?

GEORGE. I picked up one of Helen's magazines the other day and there was this article telling women what quality of orgasms they should have. It was called "The Big O." You know what really got to me? This was a magazine my mother used to buy for its fruit cake recipes.

DORIS. The times they are a changing, darling.

GEORGE. Too fast, too fast. Twenty, thirty years ago we had standards—maybe they were black and white but they were standards. Today—it's so confusing.

DORIS. Well, that's a step in the right direction. (*She moves to him and kisses him.*)

GEORGE. When did I suddenly become so appealing

DORIS. When you went from pompous to confused. (*She sits on his knee.*) Tell me, sir, what's your pleasure? A walk on the beach, dinner, or me?

GEORGE. You.

DORIS. Gee, I thought you'd never ask.

GEORGE. Doris—you're not wearing a bra!

DORIS. Oh, George, you're so forties.

GEORGE. I'm an old fashioned man.

DORIS. The next thing you'll be telling me you voted for Goldwater.

GEORGE. I did.

DORIS. You're putting me on?

GEORGE. Of course not. (*She gets off bed, picks up shoes and crosses to sofa.*) What are you doing?

DORIS. If you think I'm going to bed with any son of a bitch who voted for Goldwater you're crazy!

GEORGE. Doris, don't do this to me! Not now!

DORIS. How could you vote for a man like that?

GEORGE. Could we discuss this later?

DORIS. No, we'll discuss it now! Why did you vote for him?

GEORGE. Because I have a son who wants to be a rock musician!!

DORIS. What kind of reason is that?

GEORGE. The best reason I can come up with in my condition!

DORIS. Well, you're going to have to do better than that.

GEORGE. Okay, he was going to end the war!

DORIS. By destroying that whole country.

GEORGE. He never said that. That's the trouble with you people. You never listen.

DORIS. It's a civil war. We have no right being there in the first place.

GEORGE. Oh, I'm sick of hearing all that liberal crap! We've got the bomb. Why don't we use it!

DORIS. Are you serious?

GEORGE. Yes, I'm serious. Wipe the sons of bitches off the face of the earth!

DORIS. I don't know anything about you. What kind of a man are you?

GEORGE. Right now—very frustrated.

DORIS. All this time I thought I was going to bed with a Liberal Democrat. You told me you worked for Stevenson.

GEORGE. That was years ago.

DORIS. What changed you? What happened to you?

GEORGE. I grew up.

DORIS. Yeah, well as far as I'm concerned you didn't turn out too well.

GEORGE. Let's forget it, huh?

DORIS. Forget it? How can I forget it? I mean being stuffy and—and old fashioned is one thing but being a Fascist is another.

GEORGE. I am not a Fascist!

DORIS. You're advocating mass murder!

GEORGE. Doris—drop it, okay! Just—drop it!

DORIS. You stand for everything I'm against!

GEORGE. Then maybe you're against the wrong things!

DORIS. You used to believe in the same things I do.

GEORGE. I changed!

DORIS. Why?

GEORGE. Because Michael was killed!

DORIS. Oh, my God. How?

GEORGE. He was trying to get a wounded man onto a Red Cross helicopter and a sniper killed him.

DORIS. When?

GEORGE. We heard at a July 4th party. Helen went completely to pieces. I didn't feel a thing. I thought I was in shock and it would hit me later. It never did. The only thing I've been able to feel is blind anger. I didn't shed a tear. Isn't that something? He was my son, I loved him but—for the life of me—I can't seem to cry over him. Doris, I'm sorry about—everything.

Lately I've been a bit on edge and— It just seems to be one—damn thing—after . . . (*He starts to sob and they embrace as:*)

THE CURTAIN FALLS

END ACT TWO, Scene 1

ACT TWO

Scene 2

The Time: *A day in February, 1970.*

The Place: *The Same.*

At Rise: Doris *and* George *are sitting up in bed. She is doing a cross-word puzzle. He is reading the sports section of a newspaper. After a few moments, they put down their papers and look at each other.*

Doris. It's amazing how good it can be after twenty years, isn't it?

George. Honey, if you add up all the times we've actually made it together we're still on our honeymoon.

Doris. Did I tell you I'm a grandmother?

George. No but I think you picked a weird time to announce it. Anyway, you're the youngest looking grandmother I've ever had a peak experience with.

Doris. (*She crosses to dressing table.*) My mother thanks you, my father thanks you, my hairdresser thanks you and my plastic surgeon thanks you. (*She sits at dresser, peers into mirror, starts to brush hair and apply make-up.*) When Harry says "You're not the girl I married" he doesn't know how right he is.

George. Didn't Harry like your old nose?

DORIS. Harry thinks this is my old nose.

GEORGE. He never noticed?

DORIS. Pathetic, isn't it? A new dress I could understand—but a whole nose?

GEORGE. Well . . . (*He gets blue jeans and puts them on.*) to be totally honest I really can't see much of a difference either.

DORIS. I don't care. It's different from my side. Makes me feel more attractive.

GEORGE. Why do you feel you need a validation of your attractiveness?

DORIS. A woman starts feeling a little insecure when she gets to be forty-four.

GEORGE. Forty-five.

DORIS. See what I mean? Anyway, that's this year's bad story about Harry. Got one about Helen?

GEORGE. There was a loud party next door. Helen couldn't sleep and she didn't want to take a sleeping pill because she had to get up at six the next morning. So she stuffed two pills in her ears. During the night they melted. The next morning as the doctor was digging the stuff out of her ears he said, "You know these can be taken orally." Helen just laughed. She doesn't care.

DORIS. If that's the worst story you can tell about your wife you must be a very happy man.

GEORGE. Well, let's say I've discovered I have the potential for happiness. (*The phone rings.*)

DORIS. Hello. Oh hi Liz. No, it's sixty—not sixteen guests—that's right a brunch. We've catered a couple of parties for her before—no problem. She sets up tables around the pool and there's room for the buffet on the patio. Right. Oh, Liz, did Harry call? Okay, I'll be at this number. (*She hangs up.*) Sorry, busy weekend. I had to leave a number.

GEORGE. Does Harry know you're here?

DORIS. No, Harry still thinks I go on retreat. Don't

worry. (*She continues to make-up during the following.*)

GEORGE. I'm not worried.

DORIS. Then why are you frowning?

GEORGE. Because I'm getting bad vibes again.

DORIS. Again?

GEORGE. When you walked in I sensed your high tension level. Then after we made love I noticed a certain anxiety reduction but now I'm getting a definite negative feedback.

DORIS. When did you go into analysis?

GEORGE. How did you know I was in analysis?

DORIS. Just a wild guess. What made you start?

GEORGE. My value system changed. One day I took a look at my $150,000. house, the three cars in the garage, the swimming pool, and the gardeners. I asked myself did I really want the whole status trip? So—I decided to try and find out what I did want and who I was.

(DORIS *has gotten lounging pajamas from suitcase and exited into bathroom.*)

DORIS. (*Offstage.*) And you went from analysis to Esalen to Gestalt to Transactional to encounter groups to Nirvana.

GEORGE. Doris, just because some people are trying to widen their emotional horizons doesn't make the experience any less valid. I've learned a lot.

DORIS. (*Offstage.*) I've noticed. For one thing you learned to talk as if you're reasoning with someone about to jump off a high ledge. (*She enters and crosses to* GEORGE *for help with her zipper.*)

GEORGE. Sometimes to compensate for my former emotionalism I tend to overcompensate and tend to lose some of my spontaneity. I'm working on that.

DORIS. I'm glad to hear it. What else have you learned?

GEORGE. I've learned that behind the walls I've built

around myself I can be a very warm, caring, loving human being.

DORIS. I could have told you that twenty years ago. Tell me, how's Helen reacting to your "voyage of self-discovery"?

GEORGE. At first she tended to overreact.

DORIS. In what way?

GEORGE. She threw a grapefruit at me in the A & P. It was natural that we'd have to work through some interpersonal conflicts but now it's cool. She's into pottery. (GEORGE *sits at piano and starts to play.*)

DORIS. What do you do for a living?

GEORGE. We live very simply, Doris. We don't need much. What bread we do need I can provide by simple, honest labor.

DORIS. Like what?

GEORGE. I play cocktail piano in a singles bar in the valley. (*The phone rings again. Before answering,* DORIS *looks at* GEORGE. *He stops playing.*)

DORIS. Hello. Yes, Liz? No way. Tell him that's our final offer—I don't care how good a location it is—That's bull, Liz, he needs us more than we need him. If he doesn't like it he can shove it but don't worry—he won't. Anything else? You know where to reach me. (*She hangs up.*) I'm buying another store.

GEORGE. (*He starts playing again.*) Why?

DORIS. Money.

GEORGE. Is that why you went into business? To make money?

DORIS. No, I wanted power, too. And it finally got through my thick skull that attending C.R. groups with ten other frustrated housewives wasn't going to change anything.

GEORGE. C.R. groups?

DORIS. Consciousness raising. I take it you are for Women's Liberation?

GEORGE. Hey, I'm for any kind of liberation.

DORIS. That's a cop out and you know it. Women have always been exploited by men.

GEORGE. (*He stops playing.*) We've all been shafted, Doris, and by the same things. Look, let me lay this on you. I go to a woman doctor. The first time she gave me a rectal examination she said "Am I hurting you or are you tense?" I said "I'm tense." She said "Are you tense because I'm a woman?" and I said "No, I get tense when anybody does that to me." You see what I mean?

DORIS. I don't know but I do know that the only time a woman is taken seriously in this country is when she has the money to back up her mouth.

GEORGE. I think it's great to have a hobby.

DORIS. Hobby? We grossed over half a million the first year.

GEORGE. Honey, don't misunderstand if that's what you want I'm very happy for you. It's just that I'm not into the money thing anymore.

DORIS. Do you ever get the feeling we're drifting apart?

GEORGE. No. In many ways I've never felt closer to you.

DORIS. I don't know, sometimes I think our lives are getting—out of sync.

GEORGE. We all realize our potential in different ways at different times. As long as what you're doing gives you a sense of fulfillment, that's what's important.

DORIS. Well, I'm working on it.

GEORGE. And you have everything you want?

DORIS. With one minor exception. Somewhere along the way I seem to have lost my husband.

GEORGE. Lost him?

DORIS. Well, I don't know if I've lost him or simply misplaced him. He left home four days ago and I haven't heard from him since.

GEORGE. How do you feel about that?

DORIS. George, do me a favor—stop talking as though you're leading a human potential group. It really pisses me off.

GEORGE. That's cool.

DORIS. What's cool?

GEORGE. For you to transfer your feelings of aggression and hostility from Harry to me. As long as you know that's what you're doing.

DORIS. You know something, George? You're beginning to get on my nerves.

GEORGE. That's cool, too.

DORIS. Jesus.

GEORGE. I mean it. At least it's honest. Total honesty is the key to everything.

DORIS. Are you being totally honest with Helen?

GEORGE. I'm trying.

DORIS. Have you told her about us?

GEORGE. No—but I could. Really, I think that today she's mature enough to handle it.

DORIS. George, you're full of shit.

GEORGE. I can buy that—if you're really being honest.

DORIS. Believe me, I'm being honest!

GEORGE. But what about that garbage about "I don't know if I lost him or simply misplaced him." I mean what sort of crap is that?

DORIS. Okay, you have a point.

GEORGE. So how do you feel about all this?

DORIS. You're doing it again, George.

GEORGE. I know I'm doing it. How do you feel about this?

DORIS. Okay, I think . . .

GEORGE. No, don't tell me how you think. Tell me how you feel.

DORIS. Like I've been kicked in the stomach.

GEORGE. That's good. What else?

DORIS. Angry, hurt, betrayed and—okay, a little guilty. But, you know something? I *resent* the fact that he's making me feel guilty.

GEORGE. Why do you feel resentment?

DORIS. Look, I didn't marry Harry because he had a good head for business! Okay, it so happens that I discovered I did. Or maybe I was just lucky—I don't know. The point is, I don't love Harry any less because he's a failure as a provider. Why should he love me any less because I'm a success? At least I think that's how I feel.

GEORGE. You're not sure?

DORIS. It varies between Joan of Arc and Betty Crocker.

GEORGE. We're all going through transitional periods.

DORIS. What do I do about now?

GEORGE. Have you told him you still love him?

DORIS. Love him? Why does he think I've been hanging around for twenty-seven years?

GEORGE. I just mean that right now his masculinity is being threatened and he probably needs some validation of his worth as a man.

DORIS. And how do I do that? That's some trick.

GEORGE. Total honesty, Doris. Is it so hard for you to tell him that you understand how he feels?

DORIS. Right now—it is, yes.

GEORGE. You want him back?

DORIS. I don't know. Ask me tomorrow and I'll probably give you a different answer.

GEORGE. Why?

DORIS. Tomorrow I won't have you.

GEORGE. I'm always with you in spirit.

DORIS. Thanks a lot. It's kind of hard to put your cold feet on someone's spirit, isn't it? Especially when they're four hundred miles away.

GEORGE. Is that a proposal, Doris?

DORIS. Why, you interested?

GEORGE. Are you?

DORIS. I always thought we'd make a nice couple.

GEORGE. You didn't answer the question.

DORIS. I was the one who proposed. But don't worry, I was only three quarters serious.

GEORGE. Well, when you are completely serious why don't you ask me again.

DORIS. I bet you say that to all the girls.

GEORGE. No.

DORIS. Thanks.

GEORGE. Stop feeling so insecure.

DORIS. About what?

GEORGE. You're as feminine as you've always been.

DORIS. Gloria Steinem is going to hate me for this but I sure am glad you said that. I guess I'm not as emancipated as I thought, huh?

GEORGE. None of us are.

DORIS. You hungry?

GEORGE. Yes.

DORIS. Well, you're in luck because tonight our dinner is being catered by the chicest, most expensive French delicatessen in San Francisco.

GEORGE. How'd we swing that?

DORIS. The owner has a thing for you. (*She moves toward the front door.*) It's in the trunk of my car.

GEORGE. You want help?

DORIS. Yes. Set the table, light the candles, and when I come back make me laugh.

GEORGE. I'll try.

DORIS. Don't worry. If you can't make me laugh just hold my hand. (*She exits. After a few moments, the phone rings.* GEORGE *hesitates for a moment before answering.*)

GEORGE. Hello. No, she's not here right now. Who's calling, please? Harry!—Hold on a moment, please. (*He hesitates for a few minutes.*) Hello—Harry, we're two adult, mature human beings and I've decided to be totally honest with you . . . No, Doris is not here right now but I'd like to talk to you . . . I know you and Doris have been having difficulties lately and . . . We're very close friends. I've known Doris for twenty years and through her I feel as if I know you . . . Well, we've been meeting this same weekend for twenty years—The Retreat? Well, we can get into that later but first I want you to know something. She loves you, Harry—she really loves you—I just know, Harry . . . Look, maybe if I told you a story she just told me this morning it would help you understand. A few months ago Doris was supposed to act as a den mother for your ten year old daughter and her Indian guide group. Well, she got hung up at the store and was two hours late getting home. When she walked into the house she looked into the living room and do you know what she saw? A rather overweight, balding, middle aged man with a feather on his head sitting cross-legged on the floor very gravely and gently telling a circle of totally absorbed little girls what it was like to be in a World War II Japanese prison camp. She turned around, walked out, and sat in her car and thanked God for being married to a man like you . . . Are you still there, Harry? Well, sometimes married people get into an emotional strait jacket and find it difficult to express how they truly feel about each other. Total honesty is the key. Yes, I've known Doris for twenty years and I'm not ashamed to admit that it's been one of the most intimate, satisfying experiences of my life . . . My name? My name is Father Michael O'Herlihy.

CURTAIN

END OF ACT TWO, SCENE 2

ACT TWO

SCENE 3

THE TIME: *A day in February, 1975.*

THE PLACE: *The Same.*

AT RISE: DORIS *enters from the bathroom with a large bouquet of red roses which she places on the piano. She then crosses to the dressing table with her purse and books. She views her figure in the mirror trying to hold it in youthful posture. She is about to give up when the door opens and GEORGE enters. They embrace affectionately.*

GEORGE. You feel so good.

DORIS. So do you. But you *look* tired. You okay?

GEORGE. I've looked this way for years. You just haven't noticed. Anyway, I feel better now I'm here. This room's always had that effect on me.

DORIS. It never changes does it?

GEORGE. About the only thing that doesn't.

DORIS. I find that comforting.

GEORGE. Even old Chalmers is the same. He must be seventy-five by now. Remember when we first came here we called him old Chalmers. He must have been about the same age then we are now.

DORIS. That I don't find so comforting.

GEORGE. We were very young.

DORIS. Have we changed much?

GEORGE. Of course. I grew up with you. Remember the dumb lies I used to tell?

DORIS. I miss them.

GEORGE. I don't. It was no fun being that insecure.

DORIS. And what about me? Have I grown up too?

GEORGE. I have the feeling you were already grown up when I met you. Tell me something.

DORIS. Anything.

GEORGE. Why is it that every time I look at you I want to put my hands all over you?

DORIS. That's another thing that hasn't changed. You were always a sex maniac.

GEORGE. Let's see if I can get a fire going. (*He crosses to fireplace.*) You know I figured out with the cost of firewood it's cheaper to buy furniture, break it up, and burn it.

DORIS. Things that tight?

GEORGE. No, I'm okay. I've been doing some teaching at U.C.L.A.

DORIS. Music?

GEORGE. Accounting. The way things keep changing figures are still the only things that don't lie. (*She moves to pour two cups of coffee from a coffee pot on the coffee table.*) Doris, why'd you sell your business?

DORIS. How did you know that?

GEORGE. I'll tell you later. What made you do it?

DORIS. I was bought out by a chain. It was the right offer at the right time.

GEORGE. You don't miss the action?

DORIS. Not yet. I guess I'm still enjoying being one of the idle rich.

GEORGE. But what do you do with yourself?

DORIS. Oh, read, watch TV, play a little golf, visit my grandchildren—you know, all the jet set stuff.

GEORGE. I thought you loved working.

DORIS. Well, there was another factor. Harry had a heart attack. It turned out to be a mild one but he needed me at the time. Anyway, it's not as if I'm in permanent retirement. There's a local election coming up in a few months and I've been approached to run.

GEORGE. On what ticket?

DORIS. Independent.

GEORGE. Figures. Harry's okay now?

DORIS. Runs four miles a day and has a body like Mark Spitz. Unfortunately, he still has a face like Ernest Borgnine's. You want to hear a nice story about him?

GEORGE. Sure.

DORIS. When they were wheeling him out of intensive care he looked up at the doctor and said, "Doc, give it to me straight. After I get out of here will I be able to play the piano?" The doctor said, "Of course." And Harry said, "Funny, I couldn't when I came in." The thing is Harry never makes jokes but he saw how panicky I was and he wanted to make me feel better.

GEORGE. How are you and Harry . . . emotionally?

DORIS. Comfortable.

GEORGE. Comfortable?

Doris. Oh, it's not such a bad state. The word's been given a bad reputation by the young. (*She looks around.*) Where's your luggage? Still in the car?

George. I didn't bring any. I can't stay, Doris.

Doris. Why?

George. Look, I have so much to say and a short time to say it, so I'd better start. First of all, Helen's known about us for ten years.

Doris. When did you find that out?

George. Two months ago.

Doris. She never confronted you with it before?

George. No.

Doris. What made her tell you now?

George. She didn't. We have a very close friend, Connie—have I mentioned her before? Connie told me. Ten years and she never even hinted that she knew. That may be the nicest story I've ever told about her.

Doris. Your wife's an amazing woman.

George. She passed away, Doris. I lost her six months ago. It was all—very fast. I'm sorry to blurt it out like that. I just couldn't think of a—a graceful way to tell you. You okay, honey?

Doris. It's so strange. I never met Helen and I feel as if I've just lost my best friend. It's—crazy. Are the kids okay?

George. They'll survive. I don't think I could have gotten through the whole thing without them.

Doris. I just wish you'd tried to reach me.

George. I did. That's when I found out you'd sold the stores. I called and they gave me your home number. I let the phone ring four times, then I hung up. But it made me feel better knowing you were there if I needed you.

Doris. I wish you'd spoken to me.

George. I didn't want to intrude. I didn't feel I had the right.

Doris. My God, that's terrible. We should have been together.

George. I've been thinking about us a lot lately.

Everything we've been through together. The things we've shared. The times we've helped each other. Did you know we've made love a hundred and thirteen times? I figured it out on my Bomar calculator. (*He is fixing fresh cups of coffee.*) It's a wonderful thing to know someone that well. You know, there is nothing about you I don't know. It's two sugar, right?

DORIS. No, one.

GEORGE. So, I don't know everything about you. I don't know who your favorite movie stars are and I couldn't remember the name of your favorite perfume. I racked my brain but I couldn't remember.

DORIS. That's funny. It's My Sin.

GEORGE. But I do know that in twenty-four years I've never been out of love with you. I find that incredible? So what do you say Doris, you want to get married?

DORIS. (*Lightly.*) Married? We shouldn't even be doing this.

GEORGE. I'm serious.

DORIS. (*Looking at him.*) You really are, aren't you?

GEORGE. What did you think I was—just another summer romance? A simple "yes" will do.

DORIS. There's no such thing.

GEORGE. What is it?

DORIS. I was just thinking of how many times I've dreamed of you asking me this. It's pulled me through a lot of bad times. I want to thank you for that.

GEORGE. What did you say to me all those times?

DORIS. I always said "yes."

GEORGE. And you're hesitating now? (*Pause.*) Do you realize I'm giving you the opportunity to marry a man who has known you for twenty-four years and cannot walk by you without wanting to grab your ass?

DORIS. You always were a sweet talker.

GEORGE. That's because if I told you how I really felt about you it would probably sound like a medley of cliches from popular songs. Will you marry me?

DORIS. (*Pause.*) I can't.

GEORGE. Why not?

DORIS. I'm already married.

GEORGE. You feel you have to stay because he needs you?

DORIS. No it's a lot of things—affection, respect, a sense of continuity. We share all the same memories. It's—comfortable. Maybe that's what marriage is all about in the end—I don't know.

GEORGE. Will you tell me why I had to be so stupid five years ago to help you get back together? I mean why was I so damned generous?

DORIS. Because you felt the same way about Helen then as I do about Harry now. And if I hadn't gone back to Harry you might have been stuck with me permanently and you were terrified.

GEORGE. You could always see through me, couldn't you?

DORIS. That's okay. I always loved what I saw.

GEORGE. Well, I want you now.

DORIS. You can still have me once a year. Same time, same place.

GEORGE. Doris, I need a wife. I'm just not the kind of man who can live alone. I want you to marry me but when I came here I—I knew there was a chance you'd say "no." What I'm trying to say is—without you, I'll probably end up with Connie. She knows—all about you. The point is, she's not the sort of woman who would accept the situation. I suppose what I'm saying is that we'll probably never see each other again. You're trembling.

DORIS. The thought of never seeing you again absolutely terrifies me.

GEORGE. Doris, for God's sake—marry me!

DORIS. I can't. (*Pause.*)

GEORGE. I wish I could think of something that would break your heart, make you burst into tears and come away with me.

DORIS. You know us Italians. We never cry.

GEORGE. (*Going for his coat.*) I've got to catch a

plane. What time is it? (*She holds out her wrist.*) Five fifty-five?

DORIS. No, I keep my watch three hours and twenty-five minutes fast.

GEORGE. How long you been doing that?

DORIS. Twenty odd years.

GEORGE. Why would anyone do a thing like that?

DORIS. Personal idiosyncrasy.

GEORGE. Who were your favorite movie stars?

DORIS. Lon McAllister, Cary Grant, Marlon Brando and Laurence Olivier.

GEORGE. You've come such a long way.

DORIS. We both have.

GEORGE. Always keep your watch three hours and twenty-five minutes fast, huh. (*A beat.*) I can't believe this is happening to us. (*He exits quickly, shutting the door behind him.* DORIS *stands for a moment trying to absorb the shock of his departure.* DORIS *finally can contain her tears no longer. She throws herself face down on the bed. The door crashes open and* GEORGE *bursts into the room with his suitcase.*) Okay, I'm back goddamit!

DORIS. What about Connie?

GEORGE. Connie's eighty-nine years old! (DORIS *laughs.*) Look, I wanted you to marry me and I figured if you thought someone else wanted me I might stand a better chance . . . I was desperate, okay? Look, for once in my life I wanted a happy ending. Listen, I don't want to talk about it anymore. I'm back and I'm going to keep coming back every year until our bones are too brittle to risk contact. (DORIS *and* GEORGE *embrace as—*)

THE CURTAIN FALLS

THE END

PROPERTY LIST

dressing table with mirror attached
swivel stool
two bedside tables
bed: mattress, box spring, frame, carved headboard
two brown velour ottomans (one aged)
baby grand piano
straight-back chair
end table
coffee table
sofa
two slipcovers (one aged)
three cushions (two aged)
two nested end tables (both Stage Left of sofa)
four area rugs
chandelier with tan shades
three pair wall sconces with white shades
floor lamp & shade
electrical fire

Dressing:

Upstage Right shelves—
  one wooden carved bookend (top shelf)
  painted iron ship (middle shelf)
  two small tin candlesticks (bottom shelf)
  iron bird (bottom shelf)
On floor: Stage Right of large window—
  large ceramic pot
On wall: between windows—
  two ceramic plates
On sill of small window—
  large tin candlestick
On table: Stage Right of front door—
  large ceramic jug
On ledge: Upstage of fireplace—
  large tin "tree"
  small painted candlestick

Upstage Right corner of fireplace—
   wrought-iron fireplace tools
   one log
In fireplace—
   wrought-iron andirons
   one log (+ electrical fire with logs)
On ledge: Downstage of fireplace—
   black ceramic jug
On coffee table—
   small glass ashtray

Intermission Dressing:

Window seat—
   "tree-of-life" bowl
Piano—
   "Indian" blanket
Sofa—
   two throw pillows

Preset—top of show—Onstage:

Dressing table—
   make up case with
      lipstick
      prop makeup
      gloves
Bed—
   unmade with
      top & bottom sheets (preset for Act One, Scene 3 under
        bottom fitted sheet: 2nd fitted sheet and sewn-together,
        top-half of a blanket & sheet)
      4 pillows & cases
      bedspread
Dressing table stool—
   skirt
   blouse
   slip
Stage Right bed table—
   telephone
Stage Left bed table—
   thermos bottle, tray, glass
   George's watch
   cake on plate (in cupboard below)

Up Right drawers—
   Act One, Scene 2 clothes (to pack)
   undershorts (top drawer)
   George's suitcase (closed—on floor—above drawers)
Closet—
   wooden hangers
   George's Act One, Scene 2 hat & coat
Piano—
   Act One shawl
   Doris' jacket & hat
   purse with
      photo album
Sofa—
   3 throw pillows (1 on floor under coffee table, 2 on sofa
      covering pants)
   George's pants with
      wallet with photos—2 loose
   shirt
   tie
   shoes & socks
Fireplace—
   girdle (Downstage end of hearth)
   fire matches (Upstage shelf)
   gas jet—screwed in
Front door—
   closed
Bathroom door—
   ¾ open

Preset—top of show:

Offstage—Left:
(For Act One, Scene 1)
   breakfast tray with doily
   small plate & lid with toast
   small plate & lid with fruit
   coffee hottel with coffee
   cream
   cup & saucer
   paper napkin
   1 spoon
   1 fork
(For Act One, Scene 2)
   make up case with prop makeup

Doris' purse
George's hairbrush
George's suitcase (empty)
tray with champagne bottle with ginger ale
bucket
2 glasses
anniversary sign
(*For Act One, Scene 3*)
George's suitcase with Scotch bottle, pajamas, robe
tray with 2 plates, 2 forks, 2 paper napkins, 1 knife
tray with ice bucket & plastic ice, 2 glasses
Doris' small suitcase with kleenex
purse
coat
(*For Act Two, Scene 1*)
George's suitcase with Scotch bottle (Chevis), 1 prop shirt
daisy
(*For Act Two, Scene 2*)
make up case with comb, blusher, lipstick, mascara, erase,
    eyeliner (in makeup purse)
purse
Doris' watch
Doris' suitcase with lounging pajamas
knapsack
1 glass
perrier bottle
briefcase with folders, papers, pens
2 newspapers (1 crossword puzzle, 1 sports section)
eyeglasses
pencil
(*For Act Two, Scene 3*)
tray with coffee karafe & coffee, 2 cups & saucers, 2 spoons,
    2 napkins, cream & sugar
George's suitcase
2 books
Offstage Right—
stack of towels
vase with roses
Personal props—
George: cigar (Act One, Scene 2), pill bottle, key case,
    pen (Act Two, Scene 1)
five bedspreads—1 for each scene

PROP CHANGES

Act One, Scene 1 to Act One, Scene 2:
Strike—

Dressing table—
  make up case
  gloves
Upstage Right drawers—
  George's suitcase
Sofa—
  purse with photo album
  shirt & tie
Coffee table—
  breakfast tray
  slippers
Bed—
  bedspread

Set—

Dressing table—
  make up case (Downstage end)
  purse
  hairbrush
Bed—
  bedspread
Window seat—
  George's suitcase (open)
Piano—
  champagne tray
Front door—
  anniversary sign
Coffee table—
  birthday tray
Sofa—
  straighten pillows
Dressing table stool—
  move Downstage
Bathroom door—
  open a crack

Act One, Scene 2 to Act One, Scene 3:
Strike—

Dressing table—
  make up case
  purse
  champagne glass
Ottoman—
  George's suitcase
Piano—
  champagne tray & glass
Sofa—
  George's coat & hat
  Doris' gloves
Coffee table—
  birthday tray
Front door—
  anniversary sign
Bed—
  bedspread, sheets, 2 pillows

Set—

Bed—
  make—bedspread
  George's suitcase (on floor—down left corner of bed—closed)
Piano—
  tray with ice bucket & 2 glasses
Sofa—
  straighten pillows (1 Stage Right—1 Center—1 Stage Left)

Intermission:
Strike—

Bed—
  towels
  bedspread
  Doris' suitcase
Closet—
  Doris' coat
Window seat—
  George's suitcase

Piano—
  shawl
  scotch bottle
  2 glasses
Sofa—
  purse
  throw pillows

Set—

Bed—
  Act Two, Scene 1 & Act Two, Scene 2 bedspreads
  blanket
  George's suitcase (Downstage end of bed—open)
Window seat—
  tree-of-life bowl
Piano—
  2 tall glasses
  Indian blanket
Sofa—
  add old slipcover & cushion
  throw pillows
Doors—
  closed

Act Two, Scene 1 to Act Two, Scene 2:
Strike—

Dressing table—
  scotch glass
  pill bottle
  key case
  pen
Window seat—
  George's suitcase
Piano—
  scotch bottle
  daisy
Sofa—
  purse
Bed—
  bedspread

Set—

Dressing table—
make up case
purse
Doris' watch
eyeglasses
crossword puzzle
pencil
Bed—
unmake—add 2 pillows
newspaper (sports page)
Ottoman—
Doris' suitcase (open)
pivot
Window seat—
George's knapsack
George's jeans, jacket, necklace
Piano—
1 glass
perrier bottle
Coffee table—
briefcase
2 bracelets
Doris' boots (on floor—Stage Left of coffee table)

Act Two, Scene 2 to Act Two, Scene 3:
Strike—

Dressing table—
purse
crossword puzzle & pencil
Stage Left bed table—
newspaper
Bed—
bedspread, blanket, sheet
2 pillows
Window seat—
knapsack
Piano—
drinks tray
Coffee table—
briefcase, papers, folders, pencils
eyeglasses

Sofa—
  cushion

Set—

Bed—
  make—bedspread
Piano—
  2 books
  purse & gloves
Sofa—
  cushion
  brown pillow—Stage Right end
Coffee table—
  coffee tray
Front door—
  closed
Stage Left bed table—
  straighten telephone

COSTUME PLOT

Act *One—Scene 1:*

DORIS:
   2 piece aqua suit
   aqua print blouse
   white eyelet full slip
   green felt hat with aqua ribbon trim & feather
   beige pumps
   tan handbag
   beige gloves
   pink slippers

GEORGE:
   white athletic shirt
   white boxer shorts
   green corduroy jacket
   white shirt
   grey slacks
   burgundy tie
   black oxford shoes
   short black socks
   black belt

Act *One—Scene 2:*

DORIS:
   blue/black cocktail dress
   black crinoline
   black open-toed, sling-back pumps
   black bra or merry widow
   black cocktail gloves
   gold locket
   rhinestone earrings
   rhinestone bracelet

GEORGE:
   repeat Act One, Scene 1:
      grey slacks
      shoes & socks

    black belt
     athletic shirt & shorts
   pink shirt
   charcoal grey with pink dot tie
   grey felt hat
   old trench coat

Act One—Scene 3:

DORIS:
   2 piece blue maternity suit
   maternity padding
   low-heeled blue & white pumps
   white maternity slip
   blue trench coat
   navy straw handbag

GEORGE:
   good trench coat
   brown felt hat
   blue pajamas
   blue velvet robe
   white silk scarf
   blue velvet slippers

Act Two—Scene 1:

DORIS:
   blue sweatshirt
   blue jeans
   cloth handbag
   peace symbol necklace & beads
   sandals

GEORGE:
   3 piece brown pin-stripe suit
   light grey & white striped shirt
   brown oxford shoes
   brown ground tie
   brown executive-length socks
   brown belt
   white handkerchief in coat pocket

Act Two—Scene 2:

DORIS:
    leopard print caftan
    tan satin slippers
    3 piece eggplant lounging pajamas with tie
    brown suede boots
    amber bangle bracelets
    black bra

GEORGE:
    white t-shirt
    plaid boxer shorts
    blue jeans with patch
    denim jacket
    sandals
    neck medallion

Act Two—Scene 3:

DORIS:
    2 piece grey cashmere suit
    light brown silk blouse
    white full slip
    tan pumps
    brown suede & leather handbag
    brown gloves
    amber beads

GEORGE:
    oatmeal tweed pants
    red checked shirt
    brown sweater vest
    tan wallabies
    brown socks
    old trench coat
    brown corduroy jacket